Robin Hood

Series Editor: Sorrel Pitts
Text adapted by Sorrel Pitts
Illustrated by Laura Tolton

LADYBIRD BOOKS

UK | USA | Canada | Ireland | Australia
India | New Zealand | South Africa

Ladybird Books is part of the Penguin Random House group of companies
whose addresses can be found at global.penguinrandomhouse.com.
www.penguin.co.uk   www.puffin.co.uk   www.ladybird.co.uk

Penguin
Random House
UK

First published 2018
001

Copyright © Ladybird Books Ltd, 2018

Printed in China

A CIP catalogue record for this book is available from the British Library

ISBN: 978–0–241–33611–3

All correspondence to
Ladybird Books
Penguin Random House Children's
80 Strand, London WC2R 0RL

MIX
Paper from
responsible sources
FSC
www.fsc.org
FSC® C018179

Robin Hood

To download full story audio in both British and American accents, and to complete the listening activities at the back of the book, visit www.ladybirdeducation.co.uk

Contents

Characters

SAXONS

Robin Hood

Little John

Michael

Ralph

Tull

NORMANS

the Sheriff of
Nottingham

Margaret,
the sheriff's wife

Guy of
Gisbourne

Richard Malbete

Timothy

Diccon

Robert,
a squire

priest

5

CHAPTER ONE

A Message

A young **squire*** was leading some men through Sherwood Forest. A **priest** rode next to him.

"Where is the **outlaw**?" said the priest. "I've been on this horse for many hours."

"He'll find us," replied the squire.

"Stop!" someone shouted. Then, a tall man appeared. A group of men followed him.

"You must be Robin Hood," said the squire. "My name's Robert. I'm King Richard's squire. Here's a letter from him."

*Definitions of words in bold can be found in the glossary on pages 63–64

Robin took the letter.

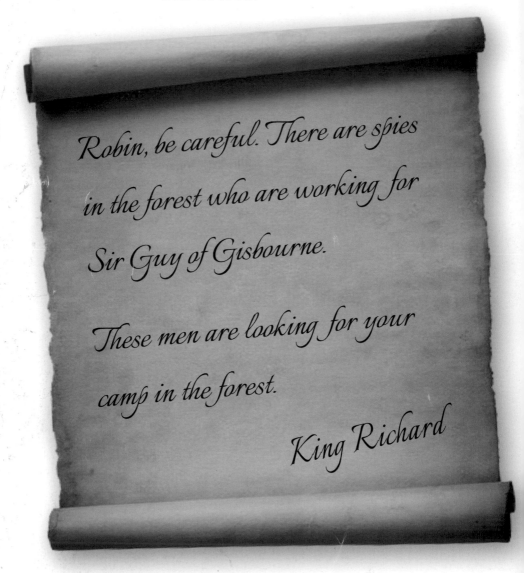

Robin, be careful. There are spies in the forest who are working for Sir Guy of Gisbourne.

These men are looking for your camp in the forest.

King Richard

"Please thank King Richard for this information," said Robin.

CHAPTER TWO

Robin is Attacked

Later that day, Robin was walking through the forest when an enormous man came out of the trees.

Robin tried to put an **arrow** in his **bow**, but the man was faster than him. He hit Robin hard with a huge **stick**, and the outlaw fell down.

"Michael! Ralph!" Robin shouted. "Help me!"

Two young men hurried to Robin, and the enormous man ran away.

"Go after him," Robin shouted, "but be careful. He may be one of Gisbourne's **spies**."

The two outlaws ran after the enormous man, and pulled him down on the ground.

"You shall explain to Robin Hood why you hit him," said Ralph.

"I have something for Robin Hood," the man shouted. Then, he threw some stones in Michael and Ralph's faces, and ran away.

CHAPTER THREE

Richard Malbete

"The man escaped, but he dropped this letter on the ground," said Michael, when the two men came back to Robin.

Then, Michael passed the letter to Robin. "You should read it first," he said.

"This letter is from Guy of Gisbourne," Robin said, and he began to read.

Dear Sheriff of Nottingham,

This is Richard Mulbete, who is a clever man. Please burn this letter when you have read it, because no one must know that he is going to work for us.

Guy of Gisbourne

"Malbete is **guilty** of many terrible crimes," Robin said. "If King Richard hears about this, he won't be happy. Malbete will be frightened now, because we have the letter."

"Malbete is a very bad man," said Michael.

"That is true," replied Robin. "We must stop him."

CHAPTER FOUR

A Plan

Robin whistled quietly, and a boy appeared. "Follow Malbete, Tull," he said. "Tell us where he goes."

"Yes, sir," said Tull.

The young outlaw ran into the forest, and Robin and the men went back to the **camp**.

"Where has Malbete gone?" Robin asked, when Tull came back.

"He's gone to Nottingham, sir," replied Tull.

"That's interesting," said Robin. "Tell me, has my friend the **potter** reached Nottingham yet?"

"No, sir," said Tull. "He's at an **inn** near to the city. He is eating and saying bad things about the **Normans**."

Robin laughed. "Ralph and Michael, please visit the potter," he said. "Tell him I want to borrow his clothes, **pots**, and horse and **cart**. I must go to the market, but I want people to think that I am him."

"We'll go to him immediately," said Michael.

CHAPTER FIVE
The Dinner

When the potter arrived at the **market square** early the next morning, it was already busy.

The potter had long hair and a thick beard, and he was wearing a hat and a coat. He stopped his cart near the sheriff's house, and quickly sold most of his pots.

Soon, he had only twelve pots left. Suddenly, the large doors to the sheriff's house opened, and the sheriff's wife, Margaret, came out.

"Good lady," said the potter, "please let me give you these pots for free."

"That's very kind," said Margaret. "You must join us for dinner this evening."

That evening, the potter was eating dinner with the Sheriff of Nottingham, his wife, and other **guests**, when an enormous man entered.

"My lord, I had a letter for you, but I lost it," said the man.

"**Liar**!" shouted the sheriff. Then he turned to some soldiers. "Take this man outside, and put him in the **stocks**," he said.

CHAPTER SIX
The Potter Loses

A little later, people talked about Robin Hood.

"He's a great **archer** who can hit a stick from fifty feet," said a man.

"That isn't true," said Timothy, a Norman, "but *I* can get close to it." He spoke to the potter. "What about you? Can you use a bow and arrow?"

"I could **shoot** well when I was young," the potter replied.

"How about going outside to shoot some arrows now?" asked the Norman.

The men went outside. The sheriff put the stick fifty feet from the two men. Timothy's arrow landed near it. Then, the potter tried, but his arrow traveled too far.

"I don't like this bow," said the potter. "Robin Hood once lent me a bow, and I shot arrows from it well."

"Do you know Robin Hood?" said the sheriff.

"Yes," replied the potter, "I can show you his camp if you want, but we mustn't leave until the sun goes down."

CHAPTER SEVEN

Into Sherwood Forest

The potter went back to the market square, where he saw Richard Malbete in the stocks. Malbete's face was red, and he was shouting at the crowds.

Later, as the sun went down, the potter led the sheriff and his men out of Nottingham and to Sherwood Forest.

Soon, the trees became thick, and the paths were difficult to follow. Suddenly, a man appeared. "Hello my friend, have you brought guests?" he said.

"I have, Little John," replied the potter. Then, he threw off his hat and coat.

"Robin Hood!" screamed the sheriff.

"Yes, it's me!" shouted Robin. "That man who you put in the stocks—he wasn't a liar, and he *did* have a letter. We know he is working for you. I brought you here so my men could go to Nottingham, and take Malbete and the letter to King Richard."

The sheriff angrily led his men away.

CHAPTER EIGHT

Normans and Saxons

"Sending that letter was stupid," the sheriff shouted at Guy of Gisbourne. "Now King Richard will be angry!"

"Robin Hood was in your house, and you let him go!" replied Gisbourne.

"I thought he was a potter," said the sheriff.

"We must catch him!" said Gisbourne. "What can we do?"

"We can have an archery competition," said the sheriff. "I'm sure Robin Hood will enter and be the winner!"

"That's a good idea!" replied Gisbourne. "Let's do it."

When Little John heard about the competition, he was worried.

"There will be Normans and **Saxons** in the competition,' he said. "The winner gets a silver arrow. They know you'll enter it, and they'll **arrest** you, Robin."

"I must go," said Robin. "But I don't want the prize. I want to beat the Normans because I am a **proud** Saxon."

CHAPTER NINE

Gisbourne is Waiting

It was the day of the archery competition. There were lots of men who carried **swords** under their coats.

"You must be careful," Little John said. "Those are the sheriff's men."

Robin nodded. He was wearing a brown coat with a **hood**. The sheriff explained the **rules**.

"Each man must try to hit a stick with his arrow. The men whose arrows are furthest from the stick will leave the competition. The stick will be moved further and further away, and the men will shoot their arrows until one man wins," he said.

While Robin was listening to the rules, a man whispered to him.

"Be careful. Gisbourne has twenty men with him. He will try to arrest you when you leave the competition," said the man.

"Thank you, my friend," replied Robin.

CHAPTER TEN

Back to Sherwood

Soon, there were only four men left in the competition. Robin and a man called Diccon were the best archers in the group.

Diccon shot his arrow. His shot was good, but Robin's was better. It hit the stick, and cut it into two pieces. Robin was the winner!

There was the sound of music, and the sheriff rose to his feet. He was holding the silver arrow.

"I arrest you, Robin Hood!" he shouted.

Then, Robin proudly threw off his coat, and all the people began to cheer.

Gisbourne and his soldiers came forward, but they could not arrest Robin because too many people stood around him.

"Let's go back to Sherwood Forest!" Robin shouted to his men.

"I'm coming with you!" shouted Diccon.

CHAPTER ELEVEN

Robin Escapes!

Robin Hood and his men got on their horses and rode away from the city, but Gisbourne and his soldiers quickly followed after them with their swords in their hands.

As they rode, Robin's men turned and shot their arrows into Gisbourne's men.

Suddenly, Little John fell—he had an arrow in his leg!

"Leave me here!" he shouted, but Diccon lifted him on to his own horse's back.

"You're coming with us!" Diccon shouted.

Robin and his men reached Sherwood Forest. Gisbourne and his men were close behind them.

Gisbourne's men were frightened, and they stopped at the edge of the forest.

"Follow them!" shouted Gisbourne, but no one wanted to ride into the dark forest.

At that moment, an arrow hit Gisbourne in the leg. He shouted, then turned his horse and rode away, with his men behind him.

"I don't think that we're going to see him again!" said Diccon.

Then, Robin and his men cheered!

Activities

The activities at the back of this book help you to practice the following skills:

🖊 Spelling and writing

📖 Reading

💬 Speaking

🎧 Listening

❓ Critical thinking

✪ Preparation for the Cambridge Young Learners exams

1 Read the information below. Choose the correct words, and write them in your notebook.

Robin Hood   Robert   priest

1   He is a squire who works for King Richard.

2   He is a person who works for a church.

3   He is an outlaw who lives in the forest.

2 Choose the correct words, and write the full sentences in your notebook.

1   A young **squire / priest** was leading some men through Sherwood Forest.

2   Then, a tall man **appeared. / disappeared.**

3   A group of men **followed / led** him.

4   Robin **gave / took** the letter.

5   "There are **spies / squires** in the forest who are working for Sir Guy of Gisbourne."

3 Match the two parts of the sentences. Write the full sentences in your notebook.

1 Later that day, Robin was walking through the forest

2 Robin tried to put an arrow in his bow,

3 The two outlaws ran after the enormous man,

a and pulled him down on the ground.

b but the man was faster than him.

c when an enormous man came out of the trees.

4 You are Robin Hood in Chapter Two. Ask and answer the questions with a friend using the words in the box.

outlaws   huge stick   ground   enormous man

1 Who attacked you?

2 What did he hit you with?

3 Who helped you?

4 Where did they pull the enormous man?

5 Read the text, and write all the text with the correct verbs in your notebook. 📖 ✏️

Dear Sheriff of Nottingham,

This . . . (**be**) Richard Malbete, who . . . (**be**) a clever man. Please . . . (**burn**) this letter when you . . . (**read**) it, because no one must . . . (**know**) that he is . . . (**work**) for us.

Guy of Gisbourne

6 Listen to Chapter Three. Describe Richard Malbete in your notebook. 🎧* ✏️

7 Read the definitions from Chapter Four.
Write the correct words in your notebook.

1 A person who is guilty of a crime,   o . . .
but has not been arrested.

2 A place where people sleep outside   c . . .
in tents.

3 A person who makes pots.   p . . .

4 People from north Europe, who   N . . .
controlled England for many years.

5 Something a person cooks food in.   p . . .

6 A small hotel where you can sleep,   i . . .
eat, and drink.

7 A large box used to hold things. It   c . . .
has wheels, and is pulled by a horse.

8 Rewrite Chapter Four as a play script.

*Robin Hood is in the forest. He whistles
quietly, and a boy appears.*

Robin: Follow Malbete, Tull. Tell us
where he goes.

9 **Read the sentences below. If a sentence is not correct, write the correct sentence in your notebook.** 📖 ✏️

1 When the potter arrived at the market square early the next morning, it was already busy.

2 The potter had short hair and a thick mustache, and he was wearing a hat and a coat.

3 Suddenly, the large doors to the sheriff's house closed, and the sheriff's wife, Margaret, went in.

4 That evening, the potter was eating dinner with the Sheriff of Nottingham, his wife, and other guests, when a small woman entered.

10 **Work with a friend. Talk about the two pictures. How are they different?** 💬 💬

a

b

In picture a, the people are outside.

In picture b, the people are inside.

11 **Read the answers below, and write the questions in your notebook.** 📖 ✏️

1 He can hit a stick from fifty feet.

2 He could shoot well when he was young.

3 They went outside.

4 It traveled too far.

5 Until the sun goes down.

12 **Listen to the definitions. Write the correct word in your notebook.** 🎧*

1 archer / liar / priest / potter / squire

2 market square / pot / stick / stocks / sword

3 arrow / bow / guest / hood / inn

4 guilty / proud / rule / shoot / spy

5 camp / stocks / Normans / sword / guilty

*To complete this activity, listen to track 14 of the audio download
available at www.ladybirdeducation.co.uk

13 **Write the sentences in the correct order.**

Suddenly, a man appeared. "Hello my friend, have you brought guests?" he said.

The potter went back to the market square, where he saw Richard Malbete in the stocks.

"I have, Little John," replied the potter, and he threw off his hat and coat.

Soon, the trees became thick, and the paths were difficult to follow.

Later, as the sun went down, the potter led the sheriff and his men out of Nottingham and to Sherwood Forest.

14 **Talk to a friend about what's happening in the picture. Ask and answer questions.**

Where are the people in the picture?

They are in Sherwood Forest.

15 Complete the text using the words from the box. Write the full text in your notebook.

> replied   shouted   thought   let

"Sending that letter was stupid," the sheriff ¹ . . . at Guy of Gisbourne. "Now King Richard will be angry!"

"Robin Hood was in your house, and you ² . . . him go!" ³ . . . Gisbourne.

"I ⁴ . . . he was a potter," said the sheriff.

16 Read page 32. Are sentences 1—5 *True* or *False*? If there is not enough information write *Doesn't say*. Write the answers in your notebook.

1 King Richard is not happy now.

2 The sheriff and Gisbourne have caught Robin Hood.

3 The sheriff wants to hold an archery competition.

4 Robin Hood will enter the archery competition.

5 Gisbourne will win the archery competition.

17 Answer the questions. Write full sentences in your notebook using the words in the box.

> arrest   sheriff   stick   twenty

1 Whose men are at the competition?

2 What must each man hit during the competition?

3 How many men are with Gisbourne?

4 What does Gisbourne want to do when Robin leaves?

18 Write some instructions in your notebook to help Robin Hood win the competition, and not be arrested.

1. Stay away from the sheriff's men.

19 Ask and answer the questions with a friend.

1 *Who won the archery competition?*

Robin Hood.

2 Did the Sheriff arrest Robin Hood?

3 Why? / Why not?

4 Where did Robin and his men want to go?

20 Write a news story about the archery competition in your notebook. 🖊️❓

ROBIN HOOD WINS
ARCHERY COMPETITION

There was a surprise at the archery competition yesterday . . .

21 **Choose the correct words, and write the full sentences in your notebook.**

1 ride	riding	rode
2 them	their	they
3 in	into	to

1 Robin Hood and his men got on their horses and . . . away from the city.

2 But Gisbourne and his soldiers quickly followed after . . . with their swords in their hands.

3 As they rode, Robin's men turned and shot their arrows . . . Gisbourne's men.

22 **Describe the characters below to a friend.** ⬤

Robin Hood The Sheriff of Nottingham Little John

Robin Hood is tall and dark, and he's got a beard. He's proud and brave . . .

Projects

23 **Look online, and find out five interesting things about Robin Hood.**

Talk to a friend. Say five things about Robin Hood that are true, and five things that are not true.

Ask your friend to guess which things are true.

Then listen to your friend, and guess which of the things they say are true.

24 This story takes place in England, during the fifteenth century. Archery was a popular sport in that time.

Find out about a popular sport in your country. Make a leaflet about it.

- What is the sport called?

- What do you do in it?

- Where is this sport played (e.g. in water, in a field, on a road)?

- How do you win?

- Is it a team sport, or do you play alone?

- Do any famous people play this sport?

25 **Write a review of this book in your notebook. Did you like it? Why? / Why not?**

In your review, include the following information:

- which character you like the most

- what part of the story you like the most

- which picture you like the most

Glossary

archer *(noun)*
a person who uses a bow
and arrows

arrest *(verb)*
when police take a
person to a police station
and keep them there,
because they believe
the person has done
something wrong

arrow *(noun)*
A thin stick with a sharp
metal end. An archer
shoots it from a bow.

bow *(noun)*
A piece of wood with a
string on it. An archer
uses it to shoot arrows.

camp *(noun)*
a place where people
sleep outside in tents

cart *(noun)*
A large box used to hold
things. It has wheels,
and is pulled by a horse.

guest *(noun)*
a person who is invited
to something (e.g. a
party, a dinner,
a wedding, etc.)

guilty *(adjective)*
When you have done
something wrong, you
are *guilty*.

hood *(noun)*
a part of a coat that you
pull up to cover your head

inn *(noun)*
a small hotel where you
can sleep, eat, and drink

liar *(noun)*
a person who lies

market square *(noun)*
a place in a town where
a market is

Normans *(noun)*
people from north
Europe, who controlled
England for many years

outlaw *(noun)*
a person who is guilty
of a crime, but has not
been arrested

pot *(noun)*
something a person
cooks food in

potter *(noun)*
a person who makes pots

priest *(noun)*
a person who works
for a church

proud *(adjective)*
to be pleased with
something about
yourself

rule *(noun)*
something that must, or
must not, be done

Saxons *(noun)*
people from Europe, who
lived in England a long
time ago

shoot *(verb)*
to send an arrow from
a bow

spy *(noun)*
a person who tries to
get information about
other people

squire *(noun)*
a young person who
works for a knight

stick *(noun)*
a piece of wood
from a tree

stocks *(noun)*
The feet of people who
were arrested were
sometimes put in wooden
stocks. This stopped
them escaping.

sword *(noun)*
a long, metal knife